Al volante / At the Wheel

Quiero conducir una ambulancia
I Want to Drive an Ambulance

Henry Abbot

traducido por / translated by
Eida de la Vega

ilustrado por / illustrated by
Aurora Aguilera

PowerKiDS press

New York

Published in 2017 by The Rosen Publishing Group, Inc.
29 East 21st Street, New York, NY 10010

Copyright © 2017 by The Rosen Publishing Group, Inc.

All rights reserved. No part of this book may be reproduced in any form without permission in writing from the publisher, except by a reviewer.

First Edition

Translator: Eida de la Vega
Editorial Director, Spanish: Nathalie Beullens-Maoui
Editor, English: Theresa Morlock
Book Design: Michael Flynn
Illustrator: Aurora Aguilera

Cataloging-in-Publication Data

Names: Abbot, Henry, author.
Title: I want to drive an ambulance = Quiero conducir una ambulancia / Henry Abbot.
Description: New York : PowerKids Press, [2017] | Series: At the wheel = Al volante | Includes index.
Identifiers: ISBN 9781499429398 (library bound book)
Subjects: LCSH: Emergency medical technicians–Juvenile literature. | Ambulance drivers–Juvenile literature.
Classification: LCC RC86.5 .A23 2017 | DDC 616.02/5092–dc23

Manufactured in the United States of America

CPSIA Compliance Information: Batch #BW17PK: For Further Information contact Rosen Publishing, New York, New York at 1-800-237-9932

Contenido

Ayudar a las personas	4
Conducir rápido	12
Al hospital	20
Palabras que debes aprender	24
Índice	24

Contents

Helping People	4
Driving Fast	12
To the Hospital	20
Words to Know	24
Index	24

Me gustaría conducir una ambulancia.

I want to drive an ambulance.

¿Cómo sería?

What would it be like?

Las ambulancias hacen un trabajo muy importante. Ayudan a las personas enfermas o heridas.

Ambulances are really important. They help people who are sick or hurt.

Hoy voy a conducir una ambulancia.

I'm an ambulance driver today.

Es un trabajo de mucha responsabilidad.

I have a big job to do.

Se recibe una llamada indicando que hay heridos.

Someone calls and says they're hurt.

Necesitan una ambulancia.

They need an ambulance.

Hago que la ambulancia vaya rápido.
Cuando alguien está herido, el tiempo apremia.

I make the ambulance go fast.
Time is important when someone is hurt.

Presiono un botón.

I press a button.

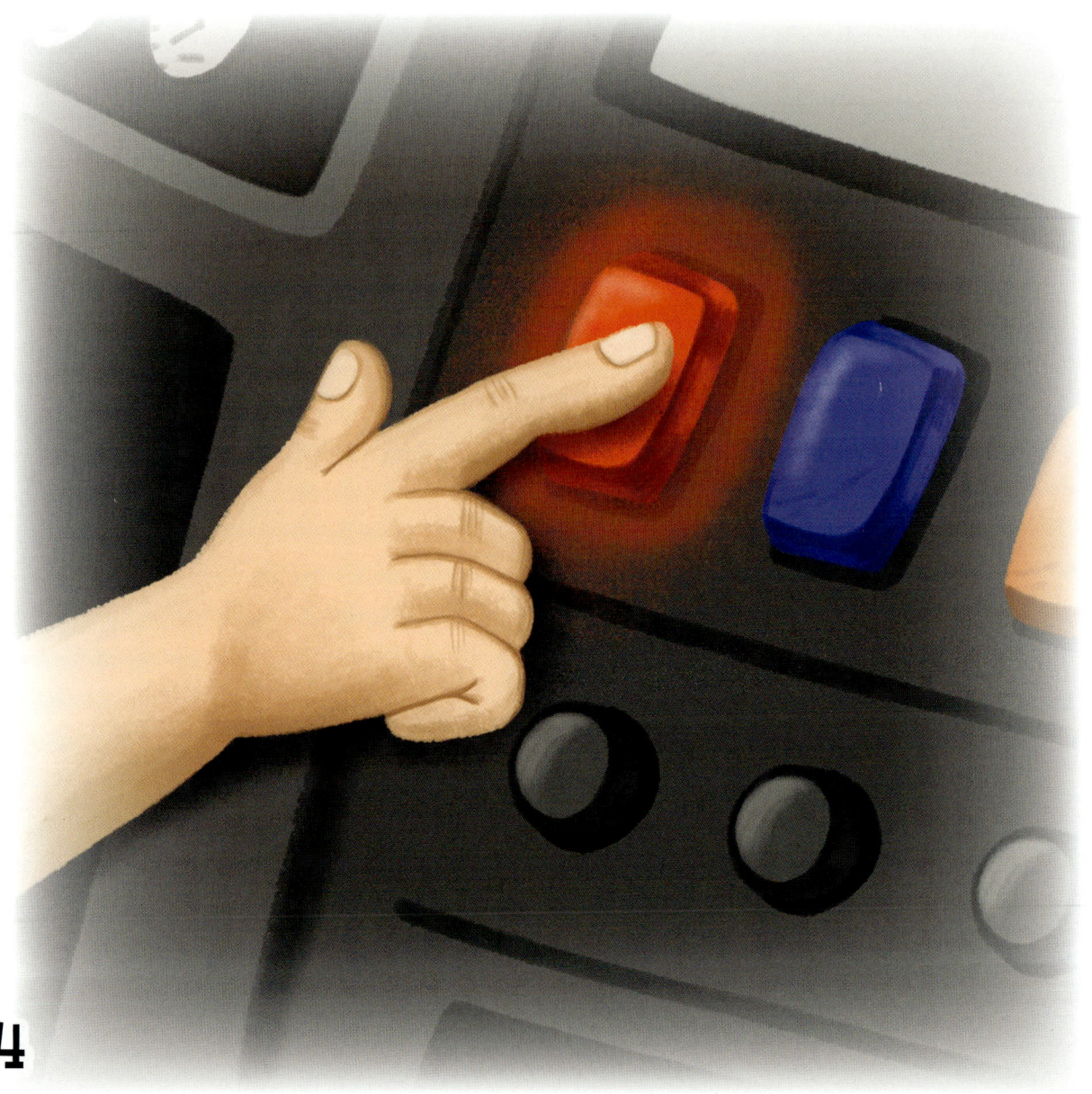

Se encienden las luces y suena la sirena.
¡La sirena hace mucho ruido!

It turns on the lights and siren. The siren is loud!

La sirena anuncia que se acerca una ambulancia.

The siren tells people an ambulance is coming.

Los otros carros se apartan del camino.

Other cars move out of the way.

¡Llegó la ambulancia!

The ambulance is here!

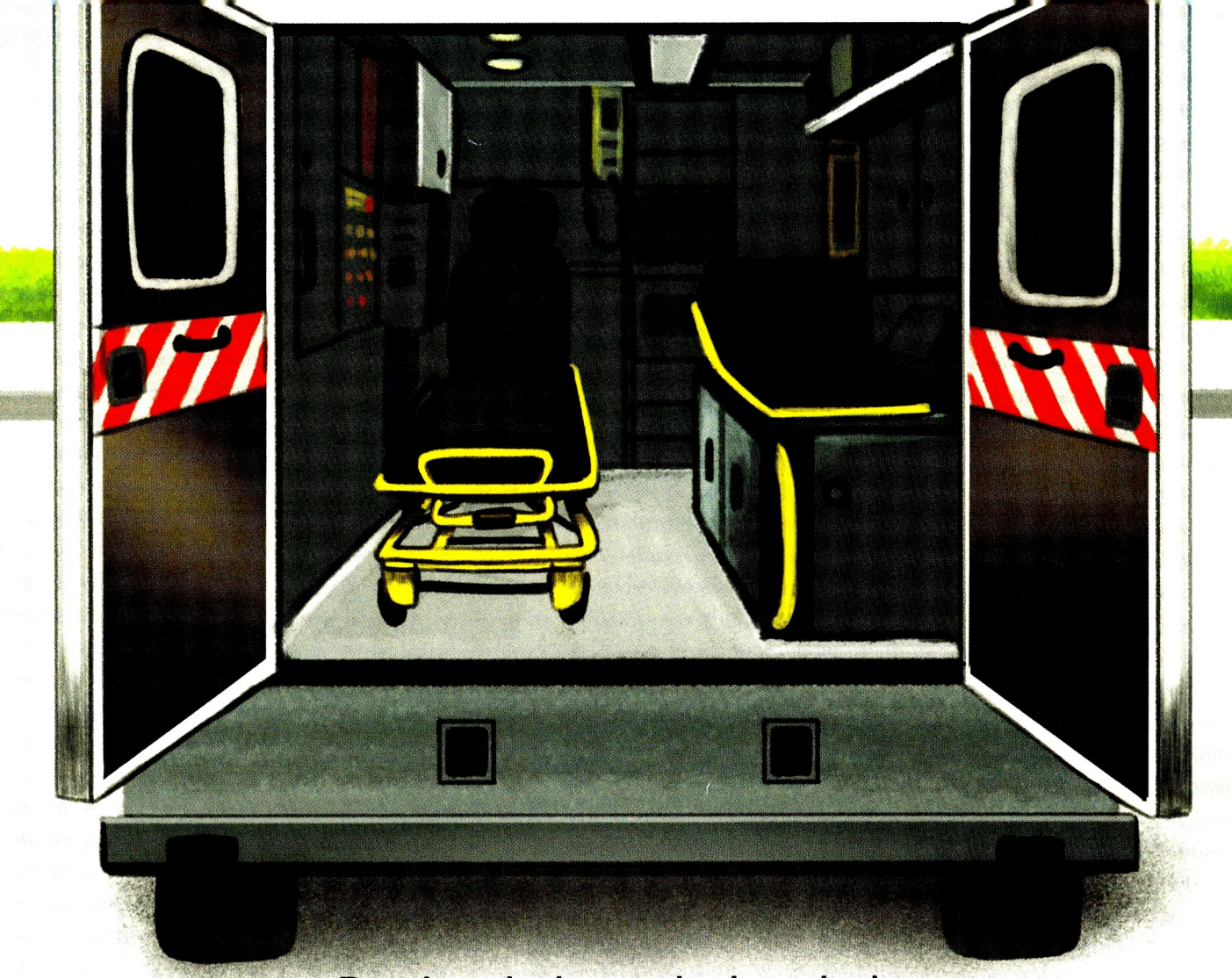

Dentro de la ambulancia hay
el equipo necesario para socorrer a las personas.

The back of an ambulance has
tools that make people feel better.

La ambulancia es suficientemente grande para transportar a las personas al hospital.

The ambulance is big enough to carry people to the hospital.

Hacia allá nos dirigimos.

We're going there next.

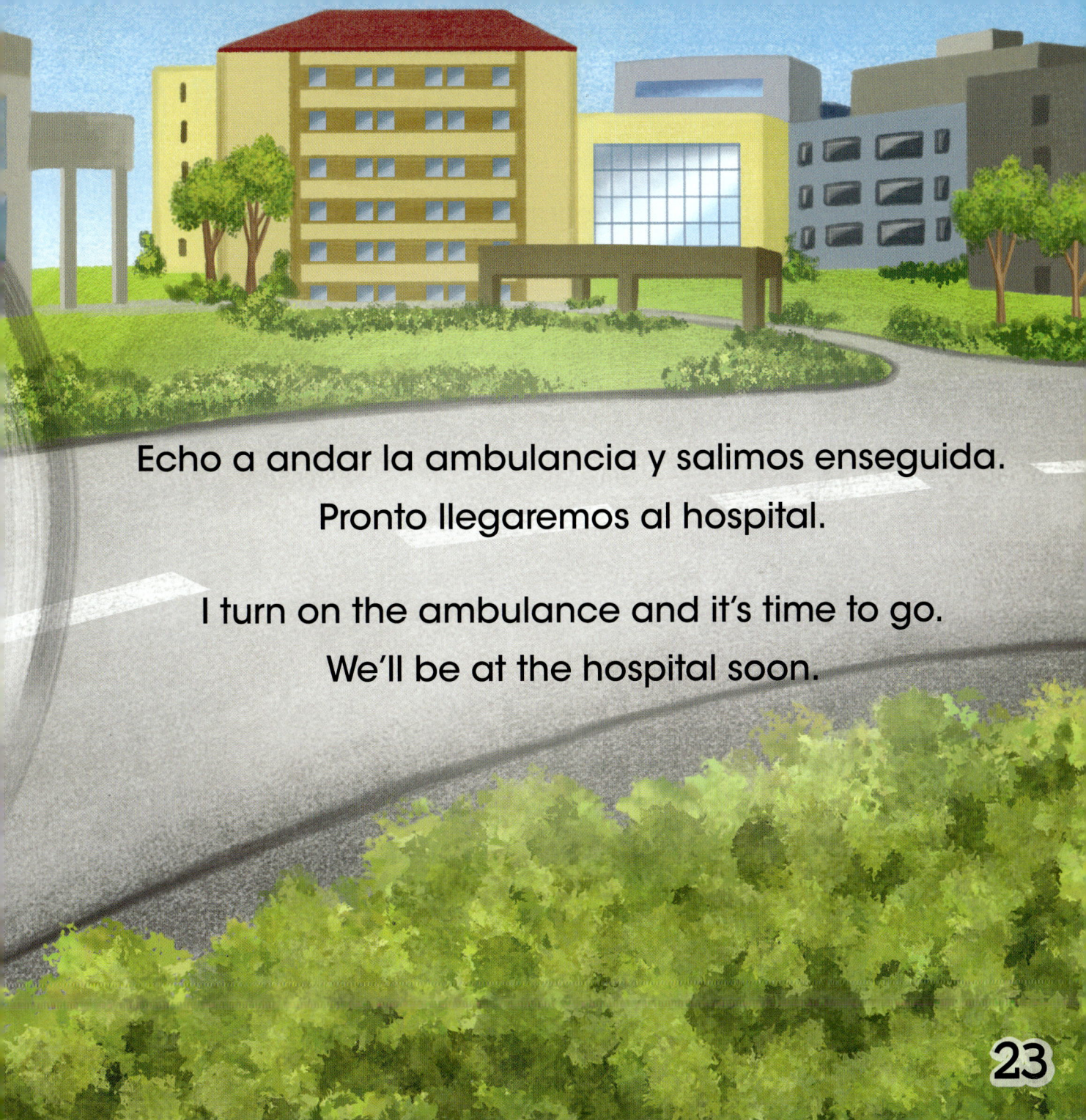

Echo a andar la ambulancia y salimos enseguida.
Pronto llegaremos al hospital.

I turn on the ambulance and it's time to go.
We'll be at the hospital soon.

Palabras que debes aprender
Words to Know

 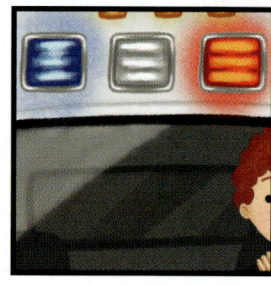 

(el) hospital (las) luces (la) sirena
hospital lights siren

Índice / Index

H
hospital/hospital, 20, 23

I
importante/important, 6, 13

L
luces/lights, 15

S
sirena/siren, 15, 16